This is George.

He was a good little monkey and always very curious.

Today was the opening of a brand-new toy store. George
and the man with the yellow hat did not want to be late.

When they arrived, the line to go inside wound all the way around the corner. When a line is this long, it's not easy for a

little monkey to be patient. George sneaked through the crowd.
All he wanted was a peek inside.

George got to the door just as the owner opened it.
"This is no place for a monkey," she said.

But George was so excited he was already inside!
Balls, dolls, bicycles, and games filled the shelves.

There were so many toys —

George didn't even know
how some of them worked.

And how about these hoops?
What did they do?

George was curious. He climbed up to pull one out of the pile.

It would not move.

George pulled harder.

Still it wouldn't move.

George pulled with all fours.

9

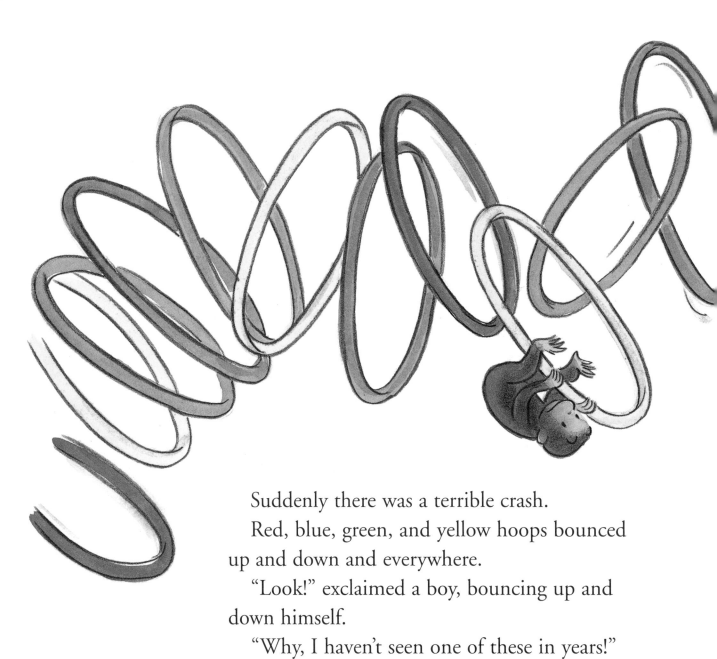

Suddenly there was a terrible crash.

Red, blue, green, and yellow hoops bounced up and down and everywhere.

"Look!" exclaimed a boy, bouncing up and down himself.

"Why, I haven't seen one of these in years!" said the boy's grandmother.

She put a hoop around her waist and gave it a spin.
George tried the hula hoop, too!

Then George pretended to be a wheel.

He rolled and rolled and. . . .

Oops! He rolled right into the owner.

The owner shook her head. "I knew you were trouble," she said. "Now you've made a mess of my new store."

Again she tried to stop George.

And again George was too quick.

In only a second he was around the corner and on the highest shelf.

Below him, George saw a little girl point to a toy out of reach. "Mommy, can we get that dinosaur?" she asked.

George picked up the dinosaur
and lowered it to the girl.

She was delighted. So was the
small boy next to her. "Could

you get that ball for me, please?"
he asked George.

George reached up, grabbed the
ball, and bounced it to the boy.

"May I have that puppet way over there?" asked another girl.

18

How lucky that George was
a monkey! He swung off the
shelf, hung on to a light, picked
up the puppet, and put it right
into her hands.

"What a show!" shouted a boy.
The children held up their new toys
and cheered. What a commotion!

Immediately the owner came running,
and then came the man with the yellow hat.
"I think we've had enough
monkey business for one day,"
the owner frowned.

Just then a girl got in the long line
to pay. "What a great store," she said.
"What a great idea to have a
little monkey helping
you," her father
told the owner.